Samuel Eaton's Day

A Day in the Life of a Pilgrim Boy

by KATE WATERS

Photographs by
RUSS KENDALL

SCHOLASTIC INC.
New York Toronto London Auckland Sydney

Many thanks to the staff and volunteers at Plimoth Plantation, particularly: Liz Lodge, Vice President of Exhibits; Carolyn Freeman Travers, Director of Research; Maureen Richard, Associate Curator; Lisa Whalen, Village Supervisor; Nanepashemet, Director of the Wampanoag Indian Program; Pat Baker, Wardrobe and Textile Manager; Kathleen Curtin, Foodways Manager; Regina Scotland, Foodways Assistant; Jill Costa, Wardrobe Associate; Carol City, Director of Public Relations; Paula Fisher, Marketing and Public Relations Associate; Marie Donlan, Receptionist; Ben Emery, Videographer; Tom Wilson, Security; Marie Pelletier, Graphics.

More thanks than we can measure to the "cast": Roger Burns, who is Samuel; Martha Sulya, who is Mam; Gary Farias, who is Samuel's father; Eric Parkman, who is Robert Bartlett; Joshua Bailey, who is Rachel; Linda Coombs and Julie Roberts, who are Penashamuk and Ammapoo; Amelia Poole, who is (again) Sarah Morton; Scott Atwood, Rick Currier, Jon Lane, Matthew Pedersen, George Sampson, David Walbridge, and Lisa Walbridge, Colonial Interpreters; Trapezious the cat; and Antic the goat.

And thanks to the supporting cast: Joy and Erin Burns; Regina Scotland (again, but this time for lending Joshua to us); Stuart Bolton and Tom Gerhardt; and David Rees, the ablest and most congenial of photographer's assistants.

To Marijka Kostiw, Associate Art Director, for making the most of our words and pictures, and to Dianne Hess, our editor, for her total involvement in this book and her support while we went about it.

Photographs on pp. 36 (John R. Ulven) and 39, courtesy of Plimoth Plantation. Woodcuts on p. 38 by Heather Saunders.

"The Marriage of Frogge and Mouse," p. 35 from *Melismata, Musicall Phansies*, by Thomas Ravenscroft. Originally published in London in 1611. Printed by William Stansby for Thomas Adams.

To Thomas Fitzgerald Weir, godson and adventurer.
—K.W.

To Roy Chaston, who lent me my first camera.
—R.K.

ISBN 0-590-48053-7

Text copyright © 1993 by Kate Waters.
Photographs copyright © 1993 by Russ Kendall.
All rights reserved. Published by Scholastic Inc.
BLUE RIBBON is a registered trademark of Scholastic Inc.

12 11 10 9 8 7 6 5 4 3 2   7 8 9/9 0/0

Printed in the U.S.A.   08

Designed by Marijka Kostiw

The photographs in this book
were taken with a Nikon F4 camera
and 20 mm, 85 mm, and 180 mm Nikkor lenses.
Some scenes were lit with Norman 400B portable lights.
Mr. Kendall used Fujichrome 50 film.

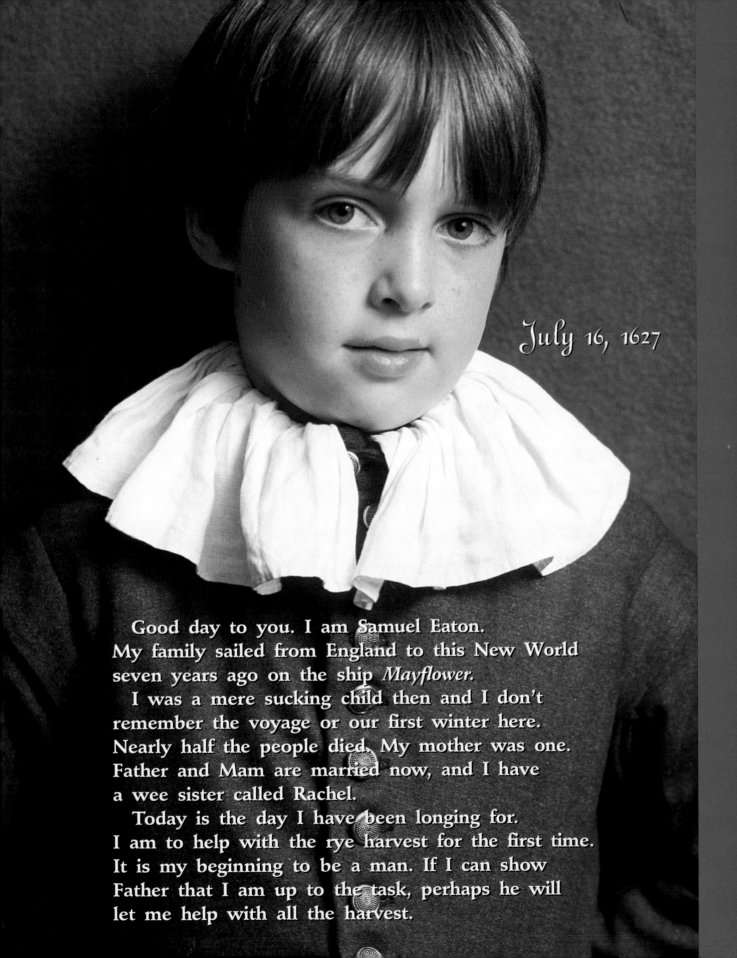

July 16, 1627

Good day to you. I am Samuel Eaton.
My family sailed from England to this New World
seven years ago on the ship *Mayflower*.

I was a mere sucking child then and I don't
remember the voyage or our first winter here.
Nearly half the people died. My mother was one.
Father and Mam are married now, and I have
a wee sister called Rachel.

Today is the day I have been longing for.
I am to help with the rye harvest for the first time.
It is my beginning to be a man. If I can show
Father that I am up to the task, perhaps he will
let me help with all the harvest.

This is our village, Plimoth Plantation.
The land was wild when we first came ashore.
My father's talents as a carpenter have been
much in demand in this new land. He has aided
in the building of all you see.

1. stockings

I am up at first light. I am so eager, I have hardly slept. I get out of bed and get dressed.

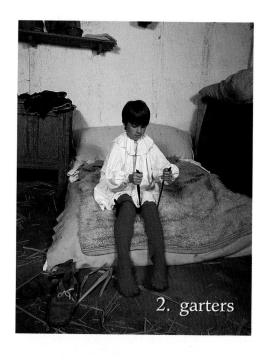

2. garters

3. breeches

4. doublet

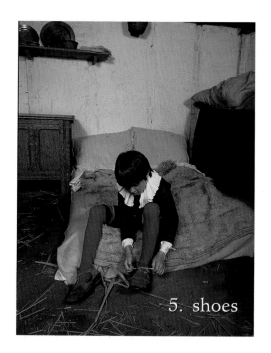

5. shoes

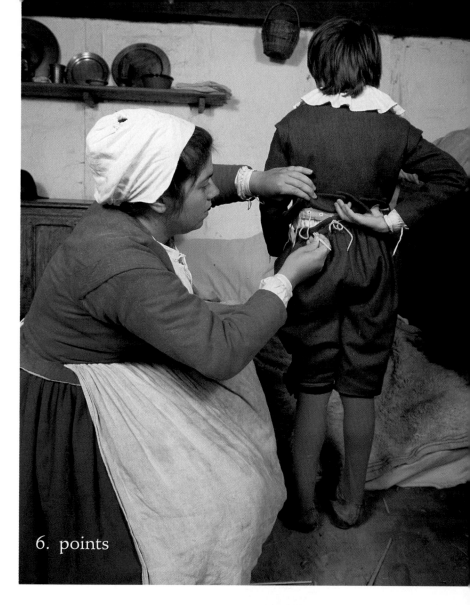

6. points

Mam helps me tie my points.

"Go then quickly now, Samuel," she says. "Thou must tend to thy labors before thou goest to the fields. And thou mustn't keep thy father waiting this morn, lest he leave thee behind."

7. hat

First, I go to the spring to fetch water. My friend Sarah Morton is out early as well. I stop for a moment, though I shouldn't. I tell her that I am glad to be aiding with the harvest and that I am afeared of being gammy at the work.

She laughs and says, "Thou art a grown boy in breeches now, Samuel, not a baby in long clothes. Thou art strong enough for the labor."

Her words send me on my way.

Now that I am almost grown, I can help catch game for the table. I run into the woods to check my snare. Father has finally let me set my own this season. It is empty this morn, but it is well placed and may soon give us a fat coney for a pottage.

I straighten the loop to set the snare again.

On the way back I gather firewood. I need to get Mam much to keep the fire while Father and I are on the rye ground.

In other seasons, Mam would go with Father to reap. Now she is not feeling well. Methinks I will have a new brother or sister!

I know that Mam will miss my help, but I'd as lief try to do a man's work this day.

Before breakfast, I brush my clothes and wash my hands and face.

Father says a blessing before we eat.

O Lord our God and heavenly Father, which of thy unspeakable mercy towards us, hast provided meate and drinke for the nourishment of our weake bodies. Grant us peace to use them reverently, as from thy hands, with thankful hearts: let thy blessing rest upon these thy good creatures, to our comfort and sustentation: and grant we humbly beseech thee good Lord, that as we doe hunger and thirst for this food of our bodies, so our soules may earnestly long after the food of eternall life, through Jesus Christ our Lord and Saviour, Amen.

I serve Father and Mam the samp.

Rachel is learning to eat upgrown food. Some goes in, but she loses somewhat by the way!

After breakfast, tis time to go. It seems to take Father a long time to be ready.

Tis no time to dally lest a summer storm come over. Our stores are low now, and all depends on getting the harvest in. We will have naught to eat this winter if we are slack and let the birds or the rains spoil the grain.

Finally we set out. Our neighbor Robert Bartlett is to help us with the harvest. He is not yet wed and has but one acre of his own. Father will share our grain in return for his labor.

As we pass through the village gate, Father tells me about his first rye harvest.

Our ground seems so vast. Since first planting, my friends and I have come out here to scare the birds and coneys away from the new plants.

Most of our ground is planted with Indian corn, and some with barley. But that will not be ready for reaping until later. The rye is ready now. Robert Bartlett says it will take but a few days to harvest the rye.

I am not grown enough to wield the sickle. It can cut a man's arm so I stay a distance behind. Father and Robert Bartlett reap the rye with the sickle and lay it behind. It is my task to gather and bind the rye.

Robert Bartlett shows me how to bind. At first I am
gammy and fall behind. To watch is easy. To do is hard.
    The straw is coarse and makes my hands smart
and my skin itch, if truth be told. And the sun burns
my neck. But I'll say narry a word. Tis but folly to
spend time in bootless complaints.

Father and Robert Bartlett sing while they cut:

It was the frog in the well, humble dum humble dum;
And the merry mouse in the mill, tweedle tweedle twino.

Tis a song with many verses and helps pass the time.
I try to join in but I am truly thinking of my empty
stomach and sore hands. Perhaps I was foolish to think
I could do a man's work!

When the sun is high I finally see Mam and Rachel coming with dinner. Of a sudden I feel small and tis a struggle not to weep. But I mustn't let Father see.

We sit under a shady tree and have bread and cheese and cold water from the spring. My legs and back ache. I am surely grateful to rest!

When Mam notices my blisters, she takes me to the brook to cool my hands.

"They will harden thy hands like a man's hands soon," she says. Mam is quiet for a time. Then she says, "Art thou faring well, Samuel? Be thou too done to remain?"

I tell her that I must remain, that I want to help bring in the rye though I truly am done. I am grateful that Mam does not fret overly and I think she will not tell Father how much I smart.

I lay down to rest by the brook.
Tis a place I could stay till morning!

Of a sudden Father is calling. He
shows me how to hone the sickle.
Then it is time to go back to the rye.

We reap and bind until the sun is setting. I have straw in my breeches and down my neck and itch all over.

My way with the rye seems harder now, not easier. But I do not fall so far behind.

At last the sun is setting.

On the way home Robert Bartlett and I stop to gather
mussels for the evening meal. They are slippery and
cling to the rocks, and the salt water stings my hands.
Penashamuk and Ammapoo are gathering as well.
We say good evening and turn towards home.

I lag behind. Then Robert Bartlett calls to me. He tells me
I worked better today than ever he did at my age. He says
he hopes someday to have a son as strong as I.
I am truly pleased and stand a bit taller.

It is nearly dark when we get home. Though I am more weary than I remember, I blow bubbles with Rachel and set her to sleep. She will always want to get in Mam's way.

Mam chops the parsley to flavor the mussels.

We eat our fill of mussels and curds.
Mam asks me about the rest of the day.

There will be no schooling for me tonight because Father has the watch. He puts on his armor, bandolier, and powder flask. I hold his musket. Of a sudden, Father asks for a word with me.

At the gate, I am quiet though I long to ask how I fared. We smell the air for rain and listen for the cries of wolves who want our cattle.

"Thou wert a fine help this day, son. Dost think thou canst keep at the harvest with the upgrown people?" Father asks.

"Oh, surely!" I say, and of a sudden the blisters and aches aren't important.

I watch as Father walks up the hill to the fort and wonder at his strength. My legs will barely take me to the house.